The Rat and the Tiger

Keiko Kasza

SCHOLASTIC INC.
New York Toronto London Auckland Sydney

ISBN 0-590-37648-9

12 11 10 9 8 7 6 5 4 3 2   8 9/9 0 1 2 3/0

Printed in the U.S.A.   14

First Scholastic printing, September 1998

Designed by Nanette Stevenson and Collen Flis.

To my parents

I'm a rat, just a tiny little rat.
Tiger is a big tough fellow.
We are best friends.
   We used to have a little problem, though. . . .

Whenever we played cowboys,
Tiger was always the good guy,
and I was the bad guy.

Tiger said, "The good guy always wins in the end."
What could I say? I'm just a tiny little rat.

Whenever Tiger and I shared a doughnut, Tiger always
cut it so that his piece was bigger than mine.

Tiger said, "It's nice to share, isn't it?"
What could I say? I'm just a tiny little rat.

Whenever Tiger saw a flower he liked,
he just pointed and expected me
to get it for him.

Then he jumped into the air and kicked my castle to pieces!

"That's it, Tiger!" I screamed.
"You're not my friend anymore.
I may be a tiny little rat
but you're a big mean bully!
Good-bye!"

I was mad. And I was sad.
But most of all, I was scared.
I had never yelled at Tiger like that before.

When Tiger found me, my heart almost stopped. I thought he might kick me just like he had kicked my castle.

"Go away, Tiger!" I shouted.

"I'm not afraid of you. Leave me alone!"

But Tiger didn't come to kick me. He had fixed my castle, and he wanted me to see it. So I did.

But I told him, "I'm still not your friend."

Then Tiger asked me if I wanted to play the good cowboy for a change. So I did.

But I told him, "I'm still not your friend."

Next, Tiger asked me if I wanted to cut our doughnut for once. So I did.

But I told him, "I'm still not your friend."

Finally, Tiger asked me if I wanted a flower. So I pointed to one, and Tiger bravely went to pick it for me.

"Maybe," I told him, "just maybe I'll be your friend again."
Tiger smiled.

Ever since that day, we have gotten along just fine.
We take turns at everything. And we split
our doughnuts right down the middle.

   We do have a little problem, though. . . .

A new kid on the block!